For Scott, treasure finder

www.dragonbloodpirates.co.uk

ORCHARD BOOKS
338 Euston Road, London NW1 3BH

First published in 2008 by Lothian Children's Books,
an imprint of Hachette Livre Australia
First published in the UK in 2010 by Orchard Books

ISBN 978 1 40830 739 7

Text © Dan Jerris 2008
Skull, crossbones and ragged parchment image © Brendon De Suza
Map illustrations on pages 4–5 © Rory Walker, 2008
All other illustrations © Orchard Books 2010

A CIP catalogue record for this book is available from the British Library.

10 9 8 7 6 5 4 3 2 1

Printed in Great Britain by J F Print Ltd., Sparkford

Orchard Books is a division of Hachette Children's Books,
an Hachette UK company.

www.hachette.co.uk

Doubloons and Disaster

Dan Jerris

ORCHARD BOOKS

Death Island

Shipwreck Island.

Cannibal Island

Sabre Island

Town

Dragon's Stomach

Snake Island

Ghost Island.

Dragon Blood Islands

Pirate Mateys and Scallywags

Alleric (Al) Breas: Lives in Drake Drive and owns a mysterious sea trunk that takes him to the Dragon Blood Islands.

Jack Seabrook: Al's best friend.

Blacktooth McGee: A very nasty pirate who runs the brigantine *The Revenge*.

Flash Johnny: Blacktooth's devious and greedy cabin boy.

Snakeboot: A magical white three-legged cat with purple eyes. Legend has it he once belonged to a terrifying pirate called Vicious Victor.

Pigface McNurt: Blacktooth's bosun; a massive pirate with a ring through his nose.

Snotty Nell: A horrible one-eyed pirate who sails a frigate called *The Tormentor*.

Grenda: Snotty Nell's daughter.

Sharkbait: Snotty Nell's one-legged bosun.

Vampire Zu: Snotty Nell's huge first mate.

Gunner: The pirate captain of the ship *The Booty*.

Mozzy: *The Booty*'s bosun (petty officer).

Slicer: *The Booty*'s cook.

Mahoot: Captain Gunner's cabin boy.

Grandfather: Mahoot's grandfather and guardian of the swimming elephants on Sabre Island.

Stanley Spong: A crooked, sneaky trader who cheats people.

Vicious Victor: A pirate ghost. He used to pillage the Dragon Blood Islands and he stole Prince Alleric's magical sabre.

Prince Alleric: The prince who once ruled Sabre Island but disappeared in mysterious circumstances.

Halimeda (Hally) Breas: Al's younger sister.

Greeny Joe: A shark so big and old that mould grows on his skin, making him glow green in the dark.

Buried Treasure

"We must be back in the Dragon Blood
Islands!" cried Alleric Breas. He was
crouched behind some sand dunes
watching a red-coated pirate. Waving
a nine-tailed whip, the pirate stood on a
wreck, which gleamed with fresh paint.
Its sails, although torn, still flapped in the
breeze. Several other pirates were pulling the
wreck apart, flinging timbers into the water.
The red pirate's voice carried in the wind.

"You sspineless layaboutss. Work fasster. Find that treasure, or it'll be the cat-o'-nine-tailss across your backss."

"At least we're on land this time," said Jack Seabrook, Al's friend. "And there's no shark."

Al shuddered at the memory of their last adventure. He and Jack had been playing in his attic at number five Drake Drive, when they had come across his grandfather's old sea trunk. They'd opened the lid and, within seconds, found themselves in the middle of the ocean. They'd been rescued by some pirates from a huge shark and survived a kidnapping before they were suddenly returned home. But now they were back again!

Al looked at the scene in front of him. "That wrecked ship looks brand new," he observed, "so something bad must have happened to the crew. We'd better be careful."

"I'm beginning to wish we'd stayed in your bedroom," said Jack. "We shouldn't have gone into the attic and opened that trunk again."

"But Snakeboot was clawing at it," said Al. He reached out and tickled the ears of the three-legged white cat beside him. "I had to see what he wanted. So when he jumped into the trunk, I looked in to see where he went. I didn't plan to come back here."

"I know," said Jack, "and I couldn't just stand there after you had disappeared. I had to follow you."

"I don't like the look of those pirates," said Al.

"Neither do I," agreed Jack. "Can we go straight back home?"

"Let's try." Al patted the cat. "Come on, Snakeboot, show us how to get back to the twenty-first century. There's a good cat."

Snakeboot seemed to understand. Purring, he headed away from the beach and the pirates. He followed a jungle path, where monkeys chattered from the trees and a large yellow snake slithered between Al's legs, making him jump. "Argh! We better keep our eyes peeled," he warned, as Snakeboot leapt ahead.

Eventually, the cat stopped in a clearing, just behind another beach. "We must be on an island," said Al, "but I don't think it's

one of the islands we visited last time, with
Captain Gunner and his crew."

Snakeboot sniffed at some freshly turned
earth in the clearing. He began to dig a hole
in the soft ground. When he was satisfied,
he squatted. "Great," said Jack. "We came all
this way just so the cat could go to the loo."

When Snakeboot finished, he scratched
the soil again, but this time unearthed
a gold coin. Al picked it up. "It's a
doubloon!" he said. "I wonder if this
is part of the treasure those pirates on
the beach are looking for?"

"I wonder what happened to the crew
of that ship?" said Jack. "Do you think the
pirates killed them?"

"I didn't see a lifeboat on the wreck," said
Al. "So if the people on the ship were being
chased by pirates, perhaps they panicked, ran
aground, abandoned ship and rowed ashore
in the lifeboat. They might have buried the

treasure and then escaped, hoping to come back some day."

"Still, finding a gold coin from some buried treasure doesn't help us get home," said Jack.

"Perhaps it can," said Al. "We can't stay here, so which way should we go? Heads, left; tails, right." He tossed the coin into the air.

"Tails," said Jack. The coin spun and dropped.

"Tails it is," said Al. "So we go right." He tossed the coin to Jack, who put it in his pocket.

Jack hoped that somehow the doubloon would bring them luck – and get them safely back home soon...

Captured by Pirates

Hours later, after walking to the right, the boys were back at the beach where they'd started – feeling tired, thirsty and hungry. The wrecked ship lay empty, the pirates nowhere to be seen. Still, the boys ducked down, crept to the edge of the beach and scanned it for any signs of danger.

Suddenly, Snakeboot's fur bristled and the cat hissed a warning. Jack and Al turned their heads. Standing behind them was a boy, about the same age as them, but a bit taller and heavier. "What are you two doing here?" he asked. His mocking grin flashed brightly.

The boys stood up to reply, but the newcomer put his hand to his mouth and called, "Hey, Blacktooth! I've just found two of the crew from the ship we've been chasing!"

In seconds, a grim band of pirates surrounded the boys. The red pirate with the whip smiled cruelly, exposing one black tooth that clung to his lower jaw. He came over and picked Al up by his collar. "By the lookss of your odd clothess, I'd guesss you've come off that foreign ssloop there," he said, pointing to the wreck.

"No, we're not from that ship," said Al, shaking his head frantically. But as soon as he spoke, Al knew he'd made a mistake.

The red pirate's face darkened in anger. "I hate liarss," he spat. He grabbed Al's arm and twisted it painfully behind his back.

"We know you had treasure on board. And we want to know where it is."

"Yeah, where is it?" the pirate boy said, pushing Jack roughly. Jack fell back onto the sand with a grunt and the gold doubloon in his pocket spilled out.

"Captain Blacktooth," the boy said as he picked up the coin, "I think we have a couple of sneaky spies here."

Blacktooth moved closer to Al and, with his stinking breath fanning Al's face, he shouted, "Where'ss the resst of your crew and where'ss the treasure?"

"It's on the other side of the island," said Jack, before Al had time to answer.

Jack and Al led the pirates to the clearing where they'd found the coin. The pirates began digging and, to their delight, soon found a sea trunk. Grinning, Blacktooth forced open the lock with the knife hanging from a sash on his chest. Inside, golden doubloons and jewellery glinted in the sunshine. "Besst day'ss work in a long time," Blacktooth said. "Pigface, you carry the chesst to the ship!"

A massive, sour-looking pirate with a ring through his nose heaved the trunk to his shoulders. Then Blacktooth studied Al and Jack for a few minutes and added, "You two liarss could be usseful. I'm sure

your family will
pay a ranssom for
you. While we
wait for them to
turn up, you can
work for me on
The Revenge."
"Or we could
sell them to Stanley
Spong," said the
boy. "He'd pay
a pretty penny
for them."
Blacktooth
smiled evilly.
"Good idea,
Flash," he
agreed. "We'd
get a reward
quicker that way."

No Escape

The pirates dragged Al and Jack on board
Blacktooth's ship, *The Revenge*, leaving
Snakeboot behind on the island. Flash, the
pirate boy, took Al and Jack down into the
bowels of the ship at knifepoint.

"I don't like you two," he told them. "I'm
the cabin boy on this ship, see. I don't
want you thinking you can just muscle in."
He pointed to a ledge in the hull of the
ship and threw two sleeping mats at them.

"You will sleep here in the bilge. And you'll get one bowl of slops a day. If you so much as even look at me or the captain, I'll make sure something unpleasant happens to you." He smiled maliciously and waved his knife. "Have you got the idea?"

Al and Jack nodded.

They weren't about to argue – Flash seemed deadly serious.

The next morning, before the sun rose, Pigface pulled Al and Jack off their sleeping mats. "You can start by cleaning the head," he told them as he shoved a bottle of putrid-smelling fluid and a bristly scrubbing brush into their hands. The head, they quickly discovered, was the pirate word for toilet. *Yuck*. But they had no choice. Once they'd finished, they washed their hands with salty water. "Pirates don't seem to have soap," said Jack sadly.

"That explains the smell," said Al.

Their fingers were red with scrubbing but their work was not done. Next, Pigface sent them to help the cook. In the galley they washed tin plates and bowls with sand and made them ready for the pirates' next meal. They thought a lot about Snakeboot, stuck on that island alone.

Flash continued to go out of his way to push and taunt the boys.

"Don't react," Al warned Jack. "He's just a big bully and he's hoping we'll get angry so he can hurt us." The boys were determined to keep their heads down and do their work. Their silence and obedience only annoyed Flash more.

It soon became obvious that the pirates were stuck: *The Revenge* swung at anchor and no wind filled the sails. Captain Blacktooth decided to dine on the poop deck. He ordered a table to be brought out and called for the treasure chest.

When Al and Jack brought the captain his meal that evening, they discovered Flash sitting beside him. Before Blacktooth ate, he pushed his bowl towards Flash. "Make it ssmaller," he said. "Lasst night I got indigesstion." He thumped his chest and burped loudly. "I've ssuffered all day."

Flash quickly took out his knife and cut Blacktooth's food into tiny pieces.

"Not ssmall enough," Blacktooth growled. "Sstart again." Anger flashed across the cabin boy's face but he cut the tiny pieces even smaller with his knife.

"Great job for a fierce pirate boy," whispered Al. "That's really knocked the smile off his face." Unfortunately his whisper carried. Flash's eyes fired up with fury and he pointed his knife at Al threateningly.

"Get on with it," snapped Blacktooth, "you're wasting time."

Flash returned to his chore but his face grew redder with anger by the minute. When the food was finally diced to Blacktooth's satisfaction, the captain began scooping it up with a silver spoon and gulping it down.

After his meal, Captain Blacktooth opened the treasure chest. He pulled out necklaces, tiaras and diamond rings, and counted the doubloons, piling them high on the table. "Happy dayss!" he cried, as he gloated over his plunder.

Flash took the opportunity to catch up with the boys. "I'll wipe that look off your face," he said. "Just you wait," and he punched Al hard on the shoulder.

"Looks like I've made a friend there," quipped Al, after Flash had gone on his way.

"I think we'd better find a way to get off this ship," Jack advised, "before things get even worse."

That night, Al and Jack decided to escape. When everyone was asleep they took their chance and crept onto the deck. The night was calm and the moon glittered brightly on the ocean. They tiptoed to the lifeboat and were untying it when a loud snore stopped them. Jack peered into the lifeboat. Pigface lay on his back beside the oars, sound asleep. They realised he would wake the minute the boat moved.

The shore, however, was tantalisingly close. Surely they couldn't give up yet? Al scanned his surroundings and spotted some loose ropes on the deck. He signalled to Jack to grab them. "We can lower ourselves down and swim to shore," he whispered.

Jack nodded in agreement.

Just as Al began to climb over the rails,
a phosphorous shape moved in the waters
below. In the bright moonlight the boys saw
a ghostly fin cut the surface. The sea rippled
in cruel silence. Al pulled himself back
onto the ship in fright. "It's Greeny Joe,"
he whispered, "the shark that nearly got us
the last time we were here!"

"I'm not risking my life," said Jack. "I'd
rather clean toilets!"

Disappointed, the boys gave up and went
back below deck.

"I just hope Snakeboot's all right," said Al.
"Somehow we have to get back to that island."

The following day, the pirates were able to
set their sails in a light wind. They had just
begun to move out to sea when another ship
was sighted. Blacktooth handed Flash an
eyeglass. "Up you go," he ordered, pointing
up the mast at the crow's nest. Flash

clambered up the ratlines and reached the small platform above the sails. "It's *The Tormentor*!" he cried from the dizzying heights, "and I think it's seen us. They're coming about!"

"*The Tormentor*?" said Al. "That means it's Snotty Nell and Grenda!"

Pirate Battle

Snotty Nell stood at the helm of *The Tormentor* as it zigzagged towards *The Revenge*.

"It's her, all right," said Jack. "You can't miss that ugly face and eye patch."

"But I can't see Grenda," said Al, scanning the ship.

Snotty Nell had her eye fixed firmly on Blacktooth, who stood near the prow. She waved her sabre angrily at him.

"Blacktooth, you beastly buccaneer!" she yelled. "I'll never forgive you! Come here so I can slice your gizzards and feed them to the sharks."

"You black-hearted harpy!" Blacktooth bellowed back. "You only got what you deserved!"

"Did I indeed?" she screamed. Green snot swung from her nose. "Well, let me give you what *you* deserve!" Her pirates raced to the gunnels, thumped their chests, rattled their swords and jeered loudly.

"Bring it on!" bawled Vampire Zu, Snotty's first mate.

"She's going to attack!" Blacktooth shouted
to his crew. "Get ready to repel. Bring *The
Revenge* a couple of pointss into the breeze."

Snotty Nell answered by trimming her
sails and bringing her ship about on a hard
tack so that the two pirate ships sailed side
by side. Some of her pirates clambered into
the rigging, some loaded pistols and others
banged their sabres on the railings. The
booming roar warned everyone that a battle
was about to begin.

On *The Revenge*, Pigface brought out
a cauldron sizzling with hot embers.
Blacktooth put long, tapered, tar-dipped
sticks into the pot, set them burning, then
gave them to his crew to put under their
tricorn hats. The fierce smouldering faces
of the men on *The Revenge* and their wild
screams curdled the blood of all who looked
at them. Blacktooth took a pistol from his
belt and fired the first shot.

Al grabbed Jack. "This could be bad," he said. The boys ducked down and ran towards the poop deck.

As the pirate ships manoeuvred in the light winds, Snotty Nell scanned Blacktooth's ship with her one good eye fixed to a spyglass. It didn't take her long to spot Blacktooth's treasure, still on the poop deck, gleaming in the sunlight. With it firmly in her sights, she twisted the frigate's wheel and broadsided *The Revenge*. The two ships collided with a shudder and splintering of wood.

Blacktooth fired his pistol again and the shot ripped through the sails on *The Tormentor*. But Snotty Nell discharged the grappling hooks. Their vicious barbs dug into Blacktooth's deck and bound the two ships together. Now, face to face, the enemies slashed at each other with their weapons. Piercing screams of anger, stunning blows of metal on metal and cries of confusion rang in the boys' ears.

Just then a rogue shot whistled past Al and thudded into the wood of the cabin wall beside him. "Get down," Jack urged, his voice shaking with fear.

Al raised his head. Above him the sails flapped thunderously and Vampire Zu leered down from the rigging. His mouth curled in a sharp-toothed grin as he focused on the treasure below. As fast as lightning he leapt from his position and, holding onto a halyard rope, swung down onto the poop deck. He grabbed the treasure trunk and, with his shipmates hauling him upwards, tried to make his escape.

Realising the treasure would be lost, Blacktooth bounded onto the deck with Flash and Pigface close behind. Blacktooth grabbed hold of Vampire Zu's feet. The wind freshened and the two ships heeled.

Refusing to relinquish his grasp, Blacktooth was hauled out over the water, with one arm around the treasure chest and the other on the halyard. The two pirates hung dangerously, rocking back and forth.

Snotty Nell left her post and ran to the bow of her ship. There, screaming in rage, she slashed at Blacktooth with her sabre. "You owe me, you scum!" she cried. "Give it up. It's mine!"

The light wind swung again, and Blacktooth jumped back on his deck. He let go of the halyard and pulled on the treasure. The halyard swung near Snotty Nell who reached out and pulled. Soon both pirate captains were fighting for the treasure in a mighty tug of war.

Flash moved quickly and climbed the mast. Edging out on the yardarm, he reached with his sword and slashed at the halyard holding Vampire Zu and the treasure.

Suddenly he stopped. He looked down into the waters below, a huge smile flashing across his face. "Snotty, you tyrant!" he screamed. "Greeny Joe is here."

Snotty looked down below her where the giant green shark waited. She jumped back in shock, letting loose an ear-splitting scream of terror. Blacktooth leapt into the air, flailing his sword at Vampire Zu's arms. Blood dropped to the deck from Vampire Zu's sliced flesh, but still he clung to the treasure.

Once again the ships heeled in the wind. Blacktooth was pulled from his standing position and Pigface grabbed onto his

captain's feet. The sudden force was too much for Vampire Zu and he let go of the treasure chest. Al and Jack leapt to their feet just in time to see the chest tip open and the bright coins glint as they tumbled downwards and out of sight.

Blacktooth landed on his backside right next to Al and Jack. Snotty Nell's screams were drowned out by Blacktooth's howls of rage. Both captains stared after the sinking treasure; below them the giant shark looked in only one direction: up at Snotty Nell.

She paled under the shark's gaze. "Get me away!" she screamed. "Get me AWAY!"

Jumping to her command, her crew quickly withdrew the grappling hooks and *The Tormentor* disengaged from *The Revenge*. Snotty flew to the helm, pulling on the wheel and jibing under the breeze. She sailed away, but not before her cannon sent one parting shot at Blacktooth's ship.

The cannonball hissed past Al's ears. Wood splintered and sprayed and a great creaking sound made Al turn and look up. The head of the foremast had split, the ropes holding it were cut and the mast spiralled downwards, hurtling towards Blacktooth. Without thinking, Al jumped up and pushed Blacktooth with all his might. The great mast crashed down, missing Blacktooth by centimetres but clipping the side of Al's head.

Al's ears were ringing as he slowly sat up and looked around. Blacktooth was also sitting up, but Flash was at his side. "You're lucky I managed to push you out of the way," said Flash, "otherwise you'd be dead!"

Blacktooth heaved himself to his knees. "Thankss, Flash," he said. "I owe you my life."

Flash smiled one of his smiles at Al, but his eyes glinted with malice. Jack leapt to his feet and was about to say something, when Al stopped him. "Shhh," he whispered. "Blacktooth would never believe us."

Jack nodded. "I know you're right, but that Flash kid really gets to me."

As Blacktooth finally got to his feet, he saw Snotty Nell's ship sailing away, a giant green fin trailing after it.

Once again, Blacktooth looked over the edge of his ship into the deep water.

The treasure would never be recovered.
"Blunderbusssess and blazing barnacless!"
he yelled, stamping his feet. He pulled at his
hair and punched the air in fury.

Flash waited a minute, and when
Blacktooth's breathing settled, he said,
"Captain, if you don't mind me saying
so, we've had nothing but bad luck since
those two came on board." He pointed
to Al and Jack. "First there was no wind,
then Snotty saw us, and then we lost

the best treasure we've had all year."

"You're right, as usual," Blacktooth said. He turned on the boys, his eyes blazing. "Pigface!" he roared. "Take thesse two vermin, row 'em ashore and leave 'em on the island." He grinned cruelly. "You two little liarss can go back where we found you. You won't last long there."

Flash's triumphant smile lit the air as Jack and Al were rowed away. "Good riddance to bad rubbish," he sneered.

Marooned

Snakeboot bounded towards the boys
as they stood on the sandy beach, watching
Pigface row away from the shore. The white
cat purred and wound himself around
their legs. "Snakeboot," said Al, "I don't
know how we're going to survive."

The cat pawed at Al's leg and turned
towards the jungle. He led them to a pool
of water, where they drank thirstily, making
cups with their hands.

Hungry, the boys hunted for fruit but had to dodge some huge pythons hanging from the trees. They made camp on the beach and Snakeboot kept guard every night. If a snake approached while they slept, he would howl loudly to warn the boys. And if one came too close, Snakeboot would move very fast; he could scare quite a few off with his strange purple eyes.

They managed to find some shellfish on the beach, which tasted terrible raw, but kept their hunger at bay. They also discovered that the lost treasure was being washed ashore by tidal currents and every day they collected more gold doubloons. It wasn't long before their pockets were full of coins.

One morning, while the boys were searching for fish, a ship approached. Fearing it might be Blacktooth, Jack and Al hid behind some sand dunes and watched.

But it wasn't *The Revenge*. It was another
ship they knew well.

The Tormentor dropped anchor in the bay
and Snotty Nell, her daughter, Grenda, and
a gang of pirates rowed ashore in a longship.
When the longship hit the sand, Vampire Zu
lifted Snotty Nell and piggybacked her ashore.
"Don't let me touch the water," she shrieked
as Vampire Zu stumbled in the lapping waves.

"You'll be fine, Mum," said Grenda,
"Greeny Joe can't smell you here."

Snotty Nell sat on the sand, wiped her nose
with the back of her hand and made herself
comfortable. "Get the sacks out of the ship,"
she ordered her crew. "You've got three hours
and I want each of you back with a full bag."
As the pirates jumped to her command, Snotty
Nell warned, "And watch out for snakes."

Curious, Al and Jack decided to follow the
crew to see what they were up to. It wasn't
long before one of the pirates stopped beside

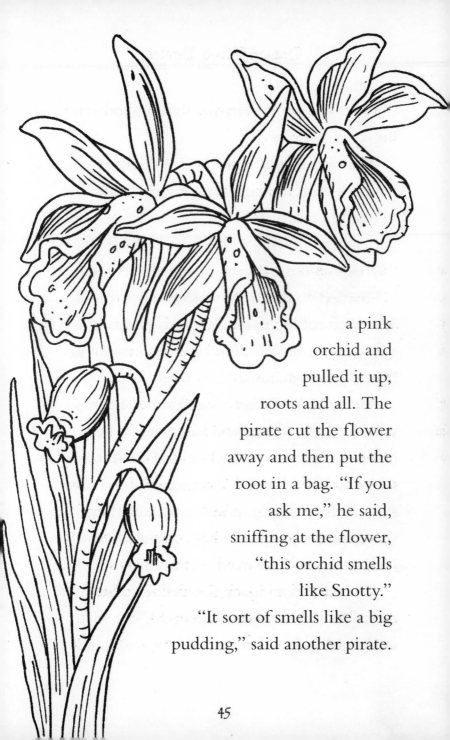

a pink
orchid and
pulled it up,
roots and all. The
pirate cut the flower
away and then put the
root in a bag. "If you
ask me," he said,
sniffing at the flower,
"this orchid smells
like Snotty."
"It sort of smells like a big
pudding," said another pirate.

45

"No wonder Greeny Joe follows her," said his mate.

Al and Jack watched them in disbelief. "What's with the pirates picking orchids?" whispered Jack.

"Hate to think," Al murmured back. "What could they want them for?"

"Sahlep," answered a voice from behind. The boys turned to find Grenda pointing a sword at them. "How did you two rascals get here?" she demanded.

Al could see Grenda wasn't too happy to see them. Last time they'd met, when her mother, Snotty Nell, had held them hostage, Al had tricked her into releasing them. Now that she had a sword pointed at them, he wasn't sure how to deal with her. Al hoped Jack could win her over.

"Blacktooth kidnapped us. Then that rotten Flash kid got us marooned," explained Jack.

Grenda shook her head in disbelief.
"Flash is a big stinker. I think I hate him
more than I hate you," she said.

"We didn't mean to get you into trouble
before," Jack said. "You don't *really* hate us,
do you?" He stood up and did a few funny
dance steps in an attempt to entertain the
pirate girl. "Look at this." He rolled
onto his back and spun around. Then he
jackknifed upwards and continued with
a few other breakdance moves.

Grenda began to giggle. "You look so silly."

"Aha, but I bet you'd like to learn a few
steps from me," Jack smiled.

Grenda smiled back and lowered her
sword. "I guess I don't hate you really."
She sat down beside them. "Were you with
Blacktooth at the big battle? Mum made me
stay down in the galley so I couldn't watch
what was going on."

"Yep," said Jack. "It was pretty dangerous.

What is it between your mum and Blacktooth? They really hate each other."

"Worse," sighed Grenda, "they want to *kill* each other. You see, Blacktooth got Mum chewed up by Greeny Joe a few years ago. They were fighting each other over this big emerald and Mum fell into the ocean during the battle. The shark was there and almost swallowed her whole. She was right inside Greeny Joe's mouth but she took her knife and jammed it into his head. The shark spat her out but she lost her eye and half her scalp, as well as the emerald."

"Wow," said Al. "Now I know why your mum took off like a crazy thing when she saw Greeny Joe!"

"But what's with the flower collecting?" asked Jack. "Your mum doesn't seem the gardening type."

Grenda giggled. "She makes this drink called sahlep. It's delicious. You grind the orchid roots up and add sugar. It smells like honey mixed with vanilla and cinnamon. Mum drinks it all the time and if we run out she goes nuts. But the orchid only grows here on Snake Island. She was on her way to collect some last week when we ran into Blacktooth."

"Do you think you could help us get off the island?" begged Jack.

"Can't," said Grenda. "Mum would have my guts for garters. Besides, you weren't very nice to me back on Death Island, remember?"

"I'm sorry," said Al, "but it was horrible being captured and tied up in the dead men's cave."

"I guess if I were you I'd have done the same thing," said Grenda, "but I still can't help you." She got up. "I'd better get back. Mum'll be looking for me."

She turned and ran off through the jungle. The boys sat down, feeling dejected. Just then a piercing scream made them leap to their feet.

"That was Grenda!" cried Jack. "We should find her." The boys raced off.

Grenda hadn't got far, but she was in a lot of trouble.

A giant golden python was squeezing her slowly, its massive coils pinning her arms and legs and crushing her lungs. Grenda's face was purple, her eyes nearly popping out.

"We've got to save her!" cried Al. "Can you get its tail, Jack?"

Jack grabbed the python's tail and heaved with all his might while Al hurled himself at the scaly monster and gripped its neck. The snake's slimy tongue flickered as it hissed furiously and whipped its tail hard, sending Jack crashing into a tree.

The creature twisted round, crushing Al into the ground. Al fought back, struggling for a foothold whilst trying to grasp the

snake's head. Snakeboot suddenly came to the rescue, jumping onto the snake's massive body and slashing at it with his claws. The python rolled, trying to hurl off its attackers. It squeezed its coils harder around Grenda, raised its massive head, opened its dripping jaws and tried to swallow her head first.

In desperation Al reached up and grabbed the python's jaws. Using all his strength he

slowly forced the snake's head away from Grenda. He pulled it down, towards himself, until finally the creature released its grip and uncoiled. Grenda took a deep, gasping breath and rolled away.

But faster than a whip, the creature recovered and reared upwards, turning on Al. It lunged and wrapped itself around Al's neck in a deathly clench. Still dazed, Jack ran over and picked up a rock. He slammed it with all his might into the snake's skull. The snake reeled back, then hissed loudly and released Al from its grip. Yellow blood dripped from the python's wound. Al wasn't taking any chances. He leapt to his feet, picked up another stone and took aim. Realising it had lost the fight, the python slithered slowly away into the jungle.

The boys helped Grenda to her feet.

"Thanks," she said. "I guess you've saved my life. I owe you. I'll try to help you get home."

"Thanks," said Al. "That's really nice of you."

"Nice?" said Grenda. "I'm not nice! I wouldn't help you at all, but I don't want to have to clean up the mess after all those snakes have squeezed you to death." She shuddered. "Just thinking about it makes me want to vomit."

"We'll walk you back to your mum," said

Al, "and we'll ask her to take us with her."

"No," said Grenda. "I'll have to smuggle you onto the ship. Mum would rather murder you than help you, especially after you stole the diamond from her. She hasn't forgiven you."

"I've got an idea," said Al. "You know the treasure that went overboard when she was fighting Blacktooth? Well, it's being washed in by the currents. It's all over the next beach." He pulled one of the coins out of his pocket to show Grenda. "We've picked up heaps. You only have to look carefully and you'll find loads of gold and jewels. If you told your mum, she'd probably head straight there to collect it all. And while she and the crew are distracted, you could row us out to the ship and hide us somewhere!"

Grenda's eyes lit up at the idea. She knew her mum would be happy that Grenda had helped her find the treasure. "It's a deal," she said, spitting on her hand. The boys spat on their hands too and they shook on it.

It wasn't long before Jack and Al, who was clutching Snakeboot to his chest, found themselves stowed away in the forecastle of Snotty Nell's ship.

Captain Gunner

Several days later *The Tormentor* docked
in town. When all was quiet, Grenda helped
Al and Jack from their hiding place near the
anchor chain and smuggled them ashore.
Once safely on the wharf, Grenda told them,
"Now don't you tell anyone what I did or I'll
never, ever speak to you again."

The boys promised and Grenda turned and
ran back to her ship. Once on deck, she gave
them a quick wave before vanishing below.

The boys looked around, not knowing
where to go. The last time they'd been on
these docks, they'd been about to sail off
on Captain Gunner's pirate ship to hunt for
treasure, but Snakeboot had led them to a
warehouse. Then suddenly they'd found
themselves back home.

Jack and Al didn't have to worry.
Snakeboot took charge. He ran along the
quay and clambered up the gangplank of a
very familiar pirate ship.

"It's *The Booty*!" cried Al. "It's Captain
Gunner's ship!"

They had just put their feet on deck when
Captain Gunner's booming voice rang out.
"WHERE HAVE YOU BEEN?" roared
the pirate. "We've been sailing back and
forth for weeks looking for you. Thought
you'd drowned!"

"Blacktooth kidapped us," said Jack, as
Slicer, the ship's cook, and their friend,

Mahoot, the cabin boy, ran onto the deck. "Luckily, we managed to escape," explained Al. Their story was almost true. "That stinking scoundrel!" cried Captain Gunner. "He was going to sell us to Spong," Jack added. "Lucky indeed that you got away then," said Captain Gunner. "We've always said you were lucky."

Gunner looked the boys up and down.
"Come with me," he said. "I've got
something for you."

He took the boys to his cabin and opened
a sea trunk. He pulled out two pairs of
pantaloons, four buckled shoes, two long
frock coats and two tricorn hats sporting
long feathers. "I can't have you wearing
foreign rubbish, so I bought you some sea
gear last time we were in port with some of
the gold you boys gave me. We hoped you
hadn't just run off and left us," he explained.

Jack and Al smiled at Captain Gunner's
generosity. "Well, we can help again," said
Jack. He emptied his pockets and Al did the
same. More than twenty gold doubloons fell
onto the floor.

"Me hearties! With this sort of money
we're gunner re-provision and sail for Sabre
Island," cried Captain Gunner happily.
"Mahoot can finally see his grandfather, the

guardian of the swimming elephants."

"Swimming elephants?" said Jack.
"I *love* elephants."

"When I lived at home, I swam with them all the time," said Mahoot.

"Even better, we can hunt for treasure hidden in the old Alleric Castle," added Slicer. "For the last fifty years every pirate has searched, but it has never been found. Only the real heir to the castle is supposed to be able to find it, but since the prince vanished mysteriously, that'll never happen."

"My grandfather is still waiting for Prince Alleric to return," said Mahoot.

"Prince Alleric?" questioned Al.

"Same name as you," said Jack. "And the same as that warehouse in town."

Mahoot looked intrigued.

"Alleric was my grandfather's name," Al explained.

"Well, *our* Prince Alleric vanished while he was chasing after Vicious Victor, the meanest pirate in the world," Mahoot informed them.

"Why was he chasing such a horrible pirate?" asked Al.

"One night, while Prince Alleric was out helping Grandfather with a sick elephant, Vicious Victor and his pirates raided his castle. They took loads of treasure, including Prince Alleric's magical sabre."

"Magical sabre?" interrupted Jack.

Mahoot looked shocked. "You haven't heard of the Dragon Blood Sabre?"

The boys shook their heads.

"The sabre is what gave our island its power. It gave the prince the power to fly anywhere in the world and gather treasure. Many people tried to steal it from him, but only Vicious Victor succeeded. After the prince lost his sabre, he sailed off hunting for Vicious Victor but was never seen again."

Al wondered if the sea trunk in his attic at home had anything to do with the magical sabre. How strange that his grandfather had the same name as the prince, and that he has such a weird sea trunk with the Dragon

Blood Islands drawn on the bottom of it? There was a mystery here, and Al would have to explore it.

"It's time to go treasure hunting," said Gunner.

Jack smiled. "When do we leave?"

Slithering Snakes
and Seaweed

The Booty set sail for Sabre Island, but the
next day black thunderheads towered over
the ocean and the water darkened before the
boys' eyes. The storm flung them furiously
through the roaring sea and the boys held on
grimly as gigantic waves crashed over them.
In desperation, the pirates pulled down the
sails before they were shredded, and fought
the storm as it drove them away from Sabre
Island. Captain Gunner and Mozzy,

the bosun, struggled with the steering and kept the ship from foundering.

Hours later, wet and exhausted, the pirates found themselves in a mass of seaweed as the storm finally died down. They shivered as they listened to the hissing of wet weed sliding in the slow swell and the slithering of thousands of eels.

"Oh, no," whispered Slicer. "I've heard about this place. It's called the Dragon's

Stomach." His whisper carried over the swishing waters.

"We're in the Dragon's Stomach!" screamed Mozzy. All the pirates paled and grabbed each other in fear.

"What's the Dragon's Stomach?" asked Al.

"They're currents," explained Mahoot. "They drag damaged ships here, swirling and trapping them until everyone is dead or the worms eat the ship and it sinks.

That's why the currents are called the Dragon's Stomach – because nothing gets out alive."

"Set the sails!" cried Gunner. "We're gunner sail out of here. No worries!" The men flew to their posts and hoisted the sails in a light breeze. *The Booty* moved, turned on itself, and sailed in a circle.

"What's wrong?" yelled Captain Gunner.

"The rudder's jammed," shrieked Mozzy. "Look, there's a massive chunk of seaweed wedged against the hull." Gunner ordered the sails to be pulled down again.

Below them the seaweed oozed and the eels wriggled. "One of us could jump over, dive down and free the rudder," suggested Jack.

"Pirates can't swim," Slicer said. "None of us have ever learnt."

"And even though we boys *can* swim, we wouldn't want one of *those* to get us," said

Mahoot, pointing to a brightly coloured sea snake wriggling through the weeds. "One bite and its venom stops you from breathing in ten seconds."

"Not more snakes!" groaned Al.

"There's got to be a way out of here," cried Captain Gunner, "or we're gunner die!"

Seaweed, snakes, eels and the slowly circling currents sent the crew into a fearful silence. "Maybe the currents will whirl us out of here," said Al, trying to brighten everyone up.

Suddenly Jack jumped to his feet. "Look, a sail!" he cried.

All eyes lifted and locked upon a strange craft as it swirled in the churning currents towards *The Booty*. Everyone shuddered as they saw, below the ship's shredded sails, a skeleton captain, standing lashed to the wheel. The rest of the crew lay dead and scattered across the deck – large hook-beaked seabirds chewed at their rotting flesh.

"We're doomed," said Slicer as he took in the gruesome sight. "Better that we jump overboard now than end up like that."

"He's right," Jack whispered to Al. "We can't just sit and wait to die."

"If we're really going to jump overboard, then I'll go first," said Al. "Give me a rope. I'll brave the snakes and have a go at that seaweed."

They didn't have much choice. Captain Gunner and Slicer lowered Al on a rope into the slimy sea. The seaweed wrapped around Al's body and clung to his legs as he entered the water. An eel brushed his skin, making him flinch. He swallowed back the tightness in his throat and concentrated on the job before him.

He had dived at the local pool back home, and had swum down into the two metre

depth to pick up things from the bottom. All
he had to do now, he told himself, was focus
on freeing up the rudder and not think about
the snakes.

He took a deep breath and exhaled. Then
he took another. Finally, he took a huge
breath and dived. He forced his eyes to open.
The salt water stung and blurred his vision,
but he could see the rudder and a large piece

of kelp jammed near the hull. Al grabbed at the kelp with both hands and pulled. Nothing happened. He pulled again and again until his lungs were bursting. He had to let go and, using the rope, he hauled himself up through the clinging seaweed to the surface, where he gasped for breath.

He prepared himself and then dived again. This time he put his feet against the hull of the ship and, using his whole body, he pulled at the kelp with all his might. Finally, the kelp burst free, spiralling out and wrapping itself around Al's waist. Quickly, Al reached for the rope and tried to hoist himself to the surface, but the kelp held him. He tried to kick his body away, but it had trapped him in a death grip.

Just as he thought his lungs would explode, he felt himself being yanked upwards. He clung to the rope for all he was worth until he emerged above the surface

with the kelp still wrapped around his body. Captain Gunner kept hauling on the rope until Al found himself safely aboard *The Booty*. "You've saved us!" cried Captain Gunner, as he pulled the strangling kelp from Al's body and wrapped him in a blanket. "Set sail and get us out of here fast," he ordered his crew. Soon, Al was warm and dry and being treated to the best dinner he could ever remember. And *The Booty* was back on track for Sabre Island.

Sabre Island

On Sabre Island stood Alleric Castle. Its marble towers and parapets reflected the morning sun. "Will you come and meet my grandfather or stay and hunt for treasure?" asked Mahoot.

"I'd rather see the elephants," Jack replied.

Al was torn. He wanted to explore the strange castle that bore his grandfather's name, but he was also curious about the elephants. "We'll explore the castle later," he decided. They left Captain Gunner at the castle door and followed Mahoot.

It wasn't long before they came to a stone temple with golden minarets. They entered the temple through a gilded door. Inside, on an altar, was a life-sized golden elephant statue, with only one emerald eye. A frail old man stood in front of the idol, lighting incense.

"Grandfather!" Mahoot cried. The old man rushed towards Mahoot and hugged him tightly. Then his eyes fell upon the boys. He pulled himself away from Mahoot and bowed low. "This is Al and Jack," said Mahoot.

"Prince Alleric?" Mahoot's grandfather said hopefully, bowing lower to Al.

"No," said Mahoot. "He's just a boy we rescued. Prince Alleric was all grown up, remember?"

"I forget," said the elderly man. "I'm getting old." He wiped a tear from his eye.

"Now then, where are my manners? Come and have a meal with me."

After dining with Mahoot's grandfather, they all went to see his elephants, which were feeding in a grove of trees. They were huge, amazing creatures. When the elephants saw Mahoot and his grandfather they trundled over and lowered their trunks. Copying Mahoot, Jack stood on one of the elephant's knees. The elephant wrapped its trunk around Jack's waist and he found himself sitting way up on a giant, wrinkly skinned elephant's back. The creature's ears flapped and a small brown eye looked up at him, as if judging him, then lifted its trunk and sniffed him. Jack patted the elephant's head, and the elephant patted Jack's leg with its trunk in return. As Jack laughed with happiness the elephants trumpeted.

"They like you," cried Mahoot happily. "How about we have a swim?"

The boys rode the elephants through the jungle towards the beach. The heat of the jungle made the sweat trickle down Al's back, and Jack's face went quite red. By the time they got to the beach, they could hardly wait to get in the water.

The elephants lowered the boys to the sand and they stripped to their underwear. Then, hanging onto the elephants' trunks, they were lifted high once again onto their backs and carried into the warm sea.

"Stay on the elephants' backs and you'll be safe from sharks," Mahoot told them.

The elephants filled their trunks with water and sprayed the boys. Screaming with laughter, they all splashed around in the water, not a shark in sight. When the afternoon sun cast long shadows, the boys left the sea and got dressed. "That was the best day of my life," declared Jack. "Thank you, Mahoot."

"Thank you," said Al to the elephants, and he bowed low. The elephants bent their giant knees and bowed back. Then, lifting their trunks, they waved goodbye and lumbered back into the jungle.

"I guess we should go to the castle now," said Jack, "and see what Captain Gunner hasn't found."

Al laughed. "And we'll let you enjoy some time with your grandfather, Mahoot. See you later."

The boys found Gunner and Snakeboot inside Alleric Castle. Murals of birds and jungle animals were painted on most of the walls. They were damaged and scratched. Al fingered a hole in the wall where an antelope was missing an eye. "Why are all the animals' eyes scratched out?" he asked.

"Us pirates took them," explained Gunner. "The eyes were emeralds, rubies and sapphires. When Prince Alleric disappeared it was fair game. Finders keepers."

"Is that why the elephant in the temple is missing an eye?" asked Jack.

"Yep," replied Gunner. "Snotty Nell took it and was cursed the minute she did. The elephant idol has terrifying powers, and if anyone harms the elephants, they're cursed."

"Is it the emerald Blacktooth wanted to steal from Snotty?" asked Al.

"That's right. Snotty wasn't called Snotty

back then. Just Nell. Ah! She was quite something to look at. In fact and I had a bit of thing for her." A goofy smile came over Gunner's face and he sighed deeply. "Her nose didn't snot at all," he added.

"But then she was attacked by Greeny Joe, right?" asked Jack.

"First, the nasty woman stole my ship," he grouched. "She sailed here and stole the emerald. Then, serve her right, Blacktooth fought her and, while they were fighting, she and the emerald fell into the ocean. Greeny Joe was right under her ship, as

usual, and he swallowed the emerald, then ripped off half her face. Now her nose for ever drips and she's ugly as sin."

"Haven't you ever tried to steal the other emerald from the idol?" Al questioned.

"No," said Gunner. "It brought Snotty no good, and only Mahoot's grandfather holds the knowledge of the emerald's powers, though legend says it opens the door to the elephants' graveyard."

"Elephants' graveyard?" Jack cried. "Wow."

"Blacktooth and Snotty would love to get their hands on the ivory from that place, I bet," said Gunner.

"Blacktooth is really mean," Al said. "It wouldn't surprise me if he came and robbed the elephant's other eye."

"He would, too," agreed Jack.

"If he did, it would break Mahoot's grandfather's heart," said Gunner. "I'm

gunner see him this evening and I will tell
him to hide the emerald. Better to be safe
than sorry. He only needs to bring it out for
his ceremonies."

"There must be tons of ivory in the
graveyard," said Jack.

"Supposed to be tons of treasure in
this castle," said Gunner, changing the
subject. "Now I'd love to get my hands
on that! You two should have a crack at
it. Someone's gunner find it, and it may
as well be us."

Al and Jack looked at each other. "Let's
explore!" said Al. He set off into the castle,
Jack and Snakeboot chasing after him.

They didn't get far before Al spied an
old painting. He stopped in front of it.
A turbaned prince, holding a sabre in one
hand, stared back at him. The sabre had
a giant ruby set in the hilt and its fine silver
blade glittered.

"That must be the magical Dragon Blood Sabre," said Jack.

"I wonder where it is now," Al mused. "I'd love to find it."

Treasure

The boys and Snakeboot had been searching
for a while. As they wandered through
the castle, Jack kicked at a pile of rubbish.
Something small and white fell out. "It's
a little elephant carved out of ivory." Jack
held out the sculpture to show Al. "Do
you think I can keep it?" he asked Al.

"I don't see why not," Al replied.
"We're hunting for treasure after all,
and that's the first thing we've found.

Let's hope we get lucky and find more."

Snakeboot interrupted their chatter by mewing. The cat's strange purple eyes gleamed knowingly and he wandered down a hallway. The boys followed. Snakeboot began to move faster and the boys had to race to keep up.

The cat tore down long hallways, through room after room, upstairs and downstairs. Finally, out of breath, the boys caught up with him in a dark hallway. Snakeboot led them through the gloom into a small room.

"How funny to have a tiny little room in a big castle," said Jack, looking around.

"It's not much larger than a cupboard," Al agreed, still puffing from their race through the maze of rooms.

"There's nothing in here," Jack sighed. "Come on, let's go. Snakeboot's just being a cat."

The boys went back to the hallway. "Which way will we go?" Jack wondered. "I'm a bit lost."

But Snakeboot pawed at one of the walls in the small room. "Snakeboot wants something," said Al. "He wouldn't have brought us in here for nothing. We should wait a minute." Al turned and studied the room further, then pointed. "Look, up near the roof!"

Painted near the ceiling, and repeated around the walls of the room, was a strange geometric design.

"It's an odd pattern, don't you think?" said Al. "It's the only pattern here and it's the same until it gets to that star on the wall over there."

"And all the other hundreds of rooms in this castle are heavily decorated, but this room isn't," said Jack. "It's certainly strange."

There was silence as Al and Jack studied the pattern.

"You know what? It isn't a pattern; it's a code," Al declared.

"Can you crack it?" asked Jack.

Al shrugged. "I can try." He stood for a few minutes and puzzled over the pattern. "I've got it," he said eventually.

He moved to the back wall and stood under the painted star, then bent down and studied the wall near the floor. He found a small depression and pressed down with his thumb. Slowly, with a loud creak, the wall moved. A secret door swung open. The boys' mouths gaped in wonder.

Snakeboot bounded through, with Jack and Al close behind. Then the secret door shut with a bang.

Before them, diamonds, pearls, sapphires and rubies glittered in mounds on the floor. On the walls hung tapestries of golden silk thread.

"It's the treasure!" cried Jack.

"Prince Alleric's lost treasure," gasped Al. He could say no more because just then his hands began to tingle. He looked across

at Snakeboot and Jack. They were fading
before his eyes.

Within seconds they were standing back
in the attic at number five Drake Drive.

"Well, we're home," said Al, "and
this time I'm certain we really were in
the Dragon Blood Islands. It wasn't our
imagination." He pointed at their clothes.
The boys were standing in the twenty-first

century in velvet frock coats, buckled shoes
and linen shirts.

"Did we really see that treasure?" asked
Jack.

"I'm not sure, to be honest," said Al. "It
might have been a mirage as we started to
disappear. We'll just have to get back to find
out! If we can find that room again it might
even give us some clues about the sabre."

They were about to discuss their plans for their next adventure when they were interrupted.

"Furgus, where are you?" It was Hally, Al's sister. "Shnookums, kitty-kitty, puss-puss! Are you up there, you naughty boy?"

"Oh, no," cried Al. "Hally is on her way up here looking for Snakeboot." The boys had no time to hide because Hally's head had already appeared above the attic stairwell.

"*There* you are," said Hally. "I've been looking for you. Come here!" The cat ran towards her obediently. Then Hally saw the boys. "Where did you get those clothes?"

Al thought quickly. "Jack's parents got us costumes so we could dress up as pirates," he lied.

"Well, you don't need Furgus for that," Hally said as she scooped Snakeboot up and carried him downstairs.

"Little does she know," winked Jack.

Clues to the Puzzle

To work out what the code on page 88 says,
use the following key:

If you're still in doubt, log on to
www.dragonbloodpirates.co.uk for the answer.

Arrr! Ahoy there, mateys!

hoist the sails and drop the anchor: ye have some treasure to find!

One swashbucklin' reader will win a haul of booty, including an Xbox console and games and an iTunes voucher, and twelve runners up will win a Dragon Blood Pirates booty bag.

For a chance to win, ye must dare to unearth the treasure using the Dragon Blood Islands map from *Death Diamond* (also available to download at www.dragonbloodpirates.co.uk), and the six big pirate stickers that are inserted in every book.

Each of the six Dragon Blood Pirates books contains a clue revealing an island protected by a dastardly pirate, and a sticker of the pirate to place on your map. When ye have solved the six clues, and have placed the six stickers, there will remain only one island, where the pirate booty be.

To win, enter online at
www.dragonbloodpirates.co.uk

Or send your name, address and the name of the island where the treasure lies to:

Dragon Blood Pirates Treasure Hunt
338 Euston Road, London NW1 3BH

Best o' luck, me hearties!

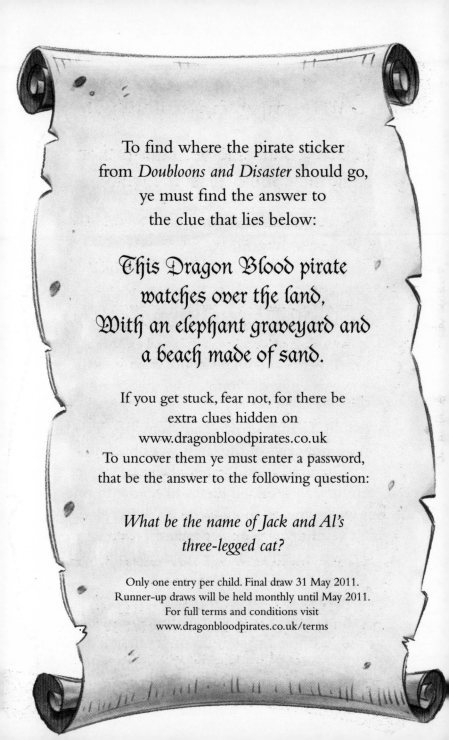

To find where the pirate sticker
from *Doubloons and Disaster* should go,
ye must find the answer to
the clue that lies below:

**This Dragon Blood pirate
watches over the land,
With an elephant graveyard and
a beach made of sand.**

If you get stuck, fear not, for there be
extra clues hidden on
www.dragonbloodpirates.co.uk
To uncover them ye must enter a password,
that be the answer to the following question:

*What be the name of Jack and Al's
three-legged cat?*

Only one entry per child. Final draw 31 May 2011.
Runner-up draws will be held monthly until May 2011.
For full terms and conditions visit
www.dragonbloodpirates.co.uk/terms

www.dragonbloodpirates.co.uk

Ahoy there shipmates!

To reel in amazin' pirate booty, steer smartly
towards www.dragonbloodpirates.co.uk

Ye'll find games, downloads, activities and
sneak previews of the latest swashbucklin'
Dragon Blood Pirates adventures.
Learn how to speak all pirate-like, how to find
out what type of pirate ye be, an' what pirate
games ye can play with yer mates! This treasure
trove is a sure feast fer yer deadlights!

Only the bravest an' heartiest amon' ye
can become a true scurvy dog, so don't
ye miss a thing and sign up to yer newsletter
at www.dragonbloodpirates.co.uk!

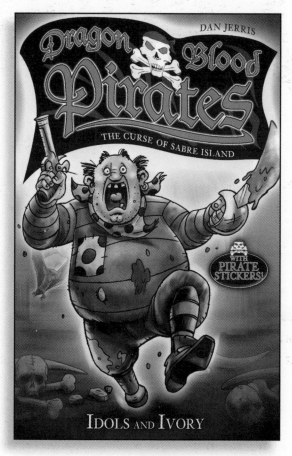

Return to Pirate Land

Alleric Breas stood in front of a dusty mirror in the attic at number five Drake Drive. He adjusted his tricorn pirate hat and dusted his blue frockcoat. "Are you ready to go back and see if that treasure was real?" he asked his best friend, Jack, remembering all the jewels and gold they'd seen as they'd left Alleric Castle on their last adventure in the Dragon Blood Islands.

Jack Seabrook sat on the floor pulling

on his black buckled shoes. He stood, put his hand in the pocket of his burgundy coat, and pulled out a small ivory elephant. He inspected it for a second, took a deep breath and announced, "I'm ready. I want to see the elephants again, too!"

Beside the boys a three-legged white cat pawed at an old sea trunk.

Al saluted. "Let's go." He reached down and patted the cat. "Snakeboot's ready to go, too."

Just as the boys stepped towards the sea trunk the attic door burst open.

A girl with curly hair, shorts and a T-shirt stood at the door. "Are you playing pirates?" asked Al's sister, Hally.

"No," said Al, "we're just standing here dressed in pirate outfits."

"Can *I* be a pirate?"

"No!" said Al. "This is a boys' game."

"I want to play!" Hally whined.

"You can't," Al grouched, "so please leave." He gave his sister a push and shut the door.

Hally heaved the door open and stuck her head back into the room. She pointed at the cat. "Furgus doesn't need to play pirates," she said. "I want him."

"You can't have him," said Al, annoyed that his sister called the cat Furgus.

"Dad! screamed Hally. "Al won't let me play pirates and he won't let me have Furgus!"

Dad's voice floated up from downstairs. "Alleric Breas! If you won't let Hally play pirates you can at least let her have the cat."

"See?" said Hally. She poked her tongue out, pushed her way into the room and scooped the cat into her arms.

When she left, Al turned to his best friend. "Do you still want to go? Snakeboot's always come with us and showed us how to get back."

"Yep," said Jack, "but I reckon if we leave the door open, Snakeboot will follow us when Hally gets sick of playing with him."

"That's true – he's a real pirate cat," Al said as he opened the attic door a crack so the cat could come in later. Then he and Jack went to the sea trunk.

If you were a fly on the wall you would

have seen two boys, dressed as pirates, open and peer inside an old trunk.

Then you would have been blinded for a second, as if a flash of bright sunlight had been reflected from a mirror. By the time your sight returned, the boys would have completely vanished.

The Elephants' Graveyard

Al and Jack found themselves squashed
behind a gold elephant's bottom. The
strong scent of incense told them they were
standing behind the idol in the Elephant
Temple on Sabre Island.

Jack's eyes lit up with pleasure. "We're
just where we wanted to be," he said. "This
is the first time we've landed somewhere
and we're not about to be eaten by a snake
or a shark!"

"Is that you, Jack?" came a voice.

The boys looked around the back of the elephant and into the temple. Mahoot, *The Booty*'s cabin boy, was there with his frail grandfather.

"Mahoot!" cried Jack happily.

"Hello," said Al politely.

The old man smiled at the boys.

"How did you get behind the idol?" asked Mahoot. "We didn't see you come in. Captain Gunner said you had vanished inside Alleric Castle and he's been a bit worried."

"We found a secret room and got lost," said Al, only telling half the truth. "Then we found ourselves here."

"Well, Gunner's sailed off to town for a few days, so Grandfather and I said we'd keep an eye out for you, and here you are!"

The boys joined Mahoot and his grandfather in front of the golden elephant idol. "Where's its eye?" asked Al, noticing

with some distress that the idol's one remaining emerald eye was missing.

"Captain Gunner suggested that I hide it," replied Mahoot's grandfather, "in case somebody tries to steal it."

"Does the emerald really help the elephants?" asked Jack.

Mahoot's grandfather nodded. "Once, the magical emerald eyes kept watch for anyone who might hurt the elephants. If the idol sensed evil from a ship sailing towards the island, a great storm would magically erupt and drive it away."

"Wow," said Al. "So how did Snotty Nell manage to steal the other eye?"

"She came for the emerald eyes, and not to hunt the elephants," answered Mahoot's grandfather. "She'd come before, to hunt the elephants, but she was overwhelmed by the power of the eyes. When she learned about the legend and the wonderful emeralds, she decided to steal them. The elephants and I caught her in the temple, and we managed to drive her away. Sadly, she took off with one of the eyes. Now there is only one eye and one power left."

"What's that?" asked Al.

"It opens the doorway to the elephants' graveyard," explained Mahoot. "The door opens when magical words are spoken, right here on the steps of the temple."

"An elephants' graveyard! Wow!" said Jack. "What happens there?"

"When the elephants are old and dying, they come to the temple. Grandfather takes them to their ancestors. For hundreds of years the elephants have known when to come," Mahoot told the boys. "When Grandfather dies, I will be the keeper of the elephants." He looked at his grandfather. "But I hope that day never comes," he added.

"It comes to us all," said Mahoot's

grandfather. "But we won't worry about such things now. Instead, I think we should all go back to my house for some tea."

Just as they were about to leave the temple, loud voices echoed from the jungle. "Many men are coming," said Mahoot's grandfather, as the noise came closer.

A louder voice carried in the wind. "The idol's eye iss in the temple."

"Hide!" Al cried, recognising the voice. But it was too late. A red-coated pirate and his fearsome crew were heading straight towards them.